W9-ANW-346

Wild About

Lowriders

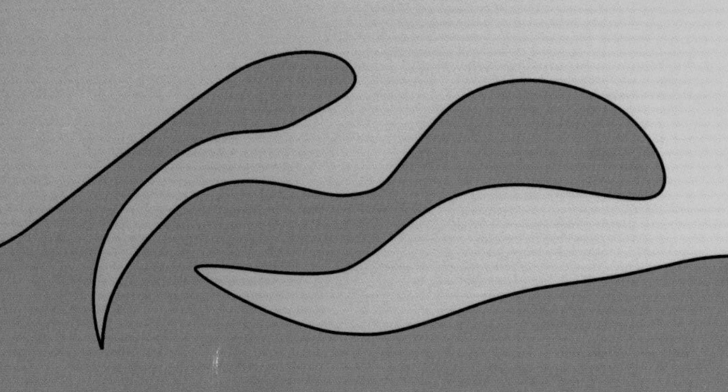

J. Poolos

PowerKiDS
press.
New York

Published in 2008 by The Rosen Publishing Group, Inc.
29 East 21st Street, New York, NY 10010

First Edition

Editor: Amelie von Zumbusch
Book Design: Greg Tucker
Photo Researcher: Nicole Pristash

Photo Credits: Cover © Robert Yager/Getty Images; pp. 5, 11, 13, 19 © Ron Kimball/Ron Kimball Stock; pp. 7, 9 © Shutterstock.com; p. 15 © Frank Micelotta/Getty Images; p. 17 © Sandy Huffaker/Getty Images; p. 21 © Matthew Peyton/Getty Images.

Library of Congress Cataloging-in-Publication Data

Poolos, Jamie.
Wild about lowriders / J. Poolos.
p. cm. — (Wild rides)
Includes index.
ISBN-13: 978-1-4042-3789-6 (library binding)
ISBN-10: 1-4042-3789-5 (library binding)
1. Lowriders—Juvenile literature. I. Title.
TL255.2.P66 2008
629.222—dc22

2006100383

Manufactured in the United States of America

Contents

Lowrider Style	4
Hydraulics	6
Flashy Cars	8
Inside Lowriders	10
Cars That Make Good Lowriders	12
Lowrider Culture	14
Car Shows and Cruising	16
Hopping and Dancing	18
Lowrider Motorcycles and Bicycles	20
Lowriders Forever!	22
Glossary	23
Index	24
Web Sites	24

Lowrider Style

A lowrider is a car or truck that has been changed so that it rides very low to the ground. Lowrider drivers use **hydraulics** to raise and lower their cars from the ground. Lowriders are fun cars. Many lowriders are built from cars made in the 1950s, but a lowrider can be made from any car.

Lowriders have flashy paint jobs, with **sparkles**, patterns, or pictures. They also have small gold or **chrome** wheels that have **spokes**. The insides of the cars are also fancy. The seats and doors are often covered with leather or a soft cloth called velvet.

Some lowriders, such as this one, are painted with brightly colored flames.

Hydraulics

Lowrider drivers use hydraulics to change how high their cars are. Hydraulics are a system of narrow tubes that join the car to its wheels. As many as 10 car **batteries** push oil through the tubes and make the car go up and down.

The driver works **switches** that control the flow of oil to each wheel. The driver raises and lowers the car by turning the switches on and off. Drivers can raise the front, back, and either side of the car. Skilled drivers make lowriders bounce, or jump up and down, in many different ways.

The driver of this lowrider is using the car's hydraulics to make it bounce.

Flashy Cars

Lowriders are built for show. The cars have special paint jobs that make them sparkle. The kind of paint used is called flake. Flake is made by mixing tiny bits of metal into the paint. Lowrider paint jobs often have flames or thin stripes called pinstripes. Some lowriders even have pictures painted on them.

Lowriders sometimes have dark windows and shiny chrome, too. The wheels on lowriders are smaller than everyday-car wheels. The wheels are small so they do not rub against the **fender** when the car is lowered. They usually have spokes and are gold or chrome colored.

You can see the chrome wheel's spokes in this close-up picture of a lowrider.

Inside Lowriders

The insides of the best lowriders are as striking as the outsides. These cars are covered in leather, velvet, and other fancy cloths inside. Some owners add pieces of wood to the **dashboards** and doors. Other owners leave the insides of their cars in their original condition.

Whether the inside of a lowrider is **customized** or not, the car usually has a special **steering** wheel. The most famous kind of lowrider steering wheel is the **chain-link** wheel. Modern lowriders also have loud radios, with booming speakers. These speakers fit into the **trunk** along with the batteries for the hydraulic system.

The inside of this lowrider is covered in red velvet.

Cars That Make Good Lowriders

Almost any car can be made into a lowrider. The original lowriders were made from cars from the 1950s, like the Mercury and the Chevrolet, or Chevy, Deluxe. Today, cars like Buicks and Cadillacs are popular choices, but the Chevy Impala is the favorite among lowrider builders.

The Chevy Impala is a two-door car from the 1960s. With its long trunk and low roof, the Impala has style. The Impala is easy to fix or customize. Large numbers of Impalas were sold, so it is still easy to find spare parts and cars that do not cost too much.

This light blue lowrider is a 1962 Chevy Impala. Impalas make great lowriders.

Lowrider Culture

Lowriders started out in **Chicano culture**. They later became part of **hip-hop** culture. When hip-hop culture became widely popular in the 1990s, more and more people became interested in lowriders. The cars were popular with both the young and the old. Today, there are lowrider clubs across the country.

Lowrider builders think of their cars as works of art. The builders and painters of the coolest lowriders are well known in lowrider culture. The makers of the best hydraulic systems, wheels, and other parts are also very respected. There are even magazines that teach people about the lowrider life.

Rappers Eminem, 50 Cent, and Dr. Dre are riding in this lowrider.

Car Shows and Cruising

One of the chief activities that lowrider clubs take part in is the car show. At car shows, lowrider builders and owners gather to show off their work. Fans come to the shows to look at the cars and to vote for their favorites. The owner of the car that is judged best in show takes home a trophy, or prize.

As any driver of a lowrider will tell you, another favorite activity is cruising. Cruising means driving a car slowly down the street. Cruising drivers make their cars bounce and show off their cool paint jobs.

These people are looking at a lowrider in a car show at the Chicano Park Heritage Festival in San Diego, California.

Hopping and Dancing

At car shows, owners also use hydraulics to lift and lower lowriders in two kinds of contests, or games people try to win. In hopping contests, each driver tries to bounce his or her car the highest. In dancing contests, drivers complete a list of moves. These moves include bouncing, turning, and lifting the corners of the car one at a time.

Some drivers sit in the driver's seat during these contests. Other drivers use switches that are connected to the car by a cable. The drivers stand beside the car and make it bounce as fans cheer them on.

Dancing is one of the most popular events at lowrider car shows.

Lowrider Motorcycles and Bicycles

Not all lowriders are cars. There are also lowrider motorcycles and bicycles. Bicycles and motorcycles do not use hydraulics, but they are low to the ground, like lowrider cars. Lowrider motorcycles have chrome and fancy, flake paint jobs. Some have pinstripes and flames.

A lowrider bicycle is a customized bicycle with a long, low seat, called a banana seat. The bicycle's wheels have many thick, shiny spokes. Lowrider bicycles also have high handlebars, which are called apehangers. Some lowrider bicycles use a chain-link steering wheel, like in a lowrider car, instead of handlebars.

This lowrider motorcycle is on show at a hip-hop car show in Hempstead, New York.

Lowriders Forever!

Lowriders are a blast to drive and show off. Their beautiful paint jobs and customized insides show us that a car can be a work of art. More and more lowrider clubs are starting all over the country. You can see lowriders cruising down the street or parked at a car show. You can even see the cars in hip-hop music videos.

It takes great skill and imagination to build a cool lowrider. As long as people enjoy bright, shiny, hopping, and dancing cars, lowriders will live forever.

Glossary

batteries (BA-tuh-reez) Things in which power is stored.

chain-link (CHAYN-lingk) Made from connected circles of metal.

Chicano (chi-KAH-noh) Having to do with Americans whose families came from Mexico.

chrome (KROHM) A shiny metal that is used on cars and motorcycles.

culture (KUL-chur) The beliefs, practices, and arts of a group of people.

customized (KUS-tuh-myzd) Made or changed to suit a certain person.

dashboards (DASH-bordz) Flat places under the big window in the front of a car.

fender (FEN-dur) A guard that goes over the wheels of a car.

hip-hop (HIP-hop) Having to do with the music and fashions of young African-Americans from cities.

hydraulics (hy-DRO-liks) A system of tubes that lift and lower the body of a car when oil is pushed through them.

sparkles (SPAHR-kulz) Things that shine in quick flashes.

spokes (SPOHKS) Rods that connect the middle of a wheel to the wheel's edge.

steering (STEER-ing) Having to do with guiding something's path.

switches (SWICH-ez) Tools used to operate a machine or control the flow of energy.

trunk (TRUNGK) The covered part in the back of a car.

Index

B
banana seat, 20
batteries, 6, 10

C
chain-link wheel, 10, 20

D
dashboards, 10
door(s), 4, 10, 12

F
fender, 8
flake, 8, 20
flames, 8, 20

H
handlebars, 20

I
Impala, 12

L
leather, 4, 10

P
paint, 4, 8, 16, 20, 22
pinstripes, 8, 20

S
seat(s), 4, 18, 20
speakers, 10
spokes, 4, 8, 20
steering wheel, 10, 20

T
trunk, 10, 12

V
velvet, 4, 10

W
wheel(s), 4, 6, 8, 10, 14, 20

Web Sites

Due to the changing nature of Internet links, PowerKids Press has developed an online list of Web sites related to the subject of this book. This site is updated regularly. Please use this link to access the list:
www.powerkidslinks.com/wild/low/